First American Edition published in 2010 by
Enchanted Lion Books LLC, 20 Jay Street, Studio M-18, Brooklyn, NY 11201
Originally published in France by les Éditions Autrement © 2005 as
Le voleur de poule by Béatrice Rodriguez
All rights reserved under International and Pan-American Copyright Conventions
A CIP record is on file with the Library of Congress
ISBN 978-1-59270-092-9
Printed in February 2010 in China by South China Printing Co., Ltd., King Yip
(Dong Guan) Printing & Packaging Factory Co.,Ltd., Daning Administrative District,
Humen Town, Dong Guan City, Guangdong Province 523930

The Chicken Thief

BÉATRICE RODRIGUEZ

ENCHANTED LION BOOKS

NEW YORK

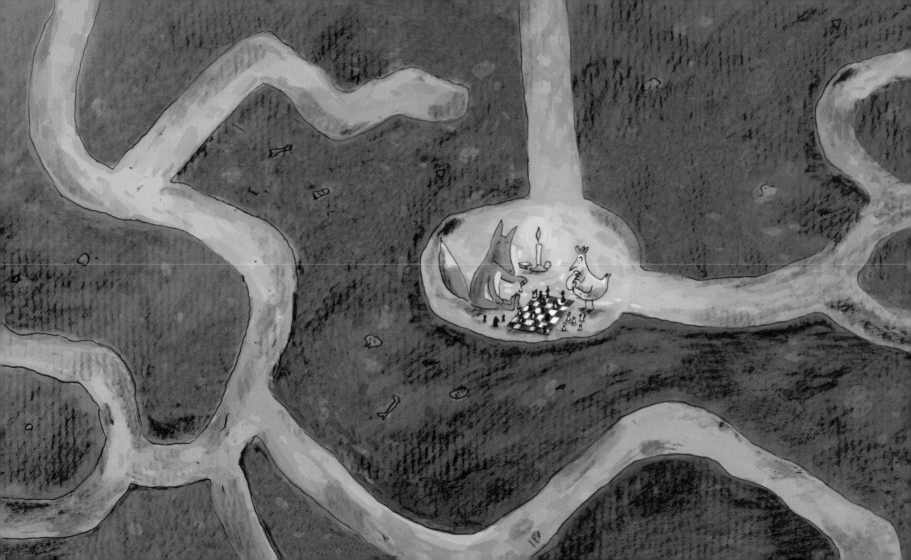